# FACING YOUR FEAR OF ADMITTING MISTAKES

BY MARI SCHUH

PEBBLE
a capstone imprint

Published by Pebble, an imprint of Capstone.
1710 Roe Crest Drive, North Mankato, Minnesota 56003
capstonepub.com

Copyright © 2023 by Capstone. All rights reserved. No part of this publication may be reproduced in whole or in part, or stored in a retrieval system, or transmitted in any form or by any means, electronic, mechanical, photocopying, recording, or otherwise, without written permission of the publisher.

Library of Congress Cataloging-in-Publication Data is available on the Library of Congress website.
ISBN: 9780756570866 (hardcover)
ISBN: 9780756571375 (paperback)
ISBN: 9780756570965 (ebook PDF)

Summary: Describes the fear of admitting mistakes and simple ways to face it.

Editorial Credits
Editor: Erika L. Shores; Designer: Dina Her; Media Researcher: Jo Miller; Production Specialist: Tori Abraham

Image Credits
Capstone Studio/Karon Dubke, 7, 8, 11, 21 (scissors, tape, stapler); Getty Images: JGI/Jamie Grill, Cover, 5, 13; Shutterstock: Africa Studio, 20 (paper), CandyRetriever, 19, Christin Lola, 15, Domira (background), cover and throughout, imtmphoto, 14, Kapitosh (cloud), cover and throughout, Marish (brave girl), cover and throughout, Pixel-Shot, 6, 18, tairome, 17

All internet sites appearing in back matter were available and accurate when this book was sent to press.

Printed and bound in China. PO5130

# TABLE OF CONTENTS

We All Make Mistakes ................................ 4

Owning Up .................................................. 8

Facing Your Mistakes ............................... 12

Doing Your Best ........................................ 18

    Thinking Rings ................................... 20

    Glossary ............................................... 22

    Read More ........................................... 23

    Internet Sites ...................................... 23

    Index ..................................................... 24

    About the Author .............................. 24

Words in **bold** are in the glossary.

# WE ALL MAKE MISTAKES

Think of a **mistake** you made. What did you do? How did you feel? What did you do next?

Everyone makes mistakes. It is a normal thing to do. Mistakes are a part of life. After all, no one is perfect. What happens after a mistake is what matters. What you say and do after a mistake is what counts.

Mistakes are made every day. Mason played wrong notes on the piano. Sam broke Atul's toy and did not tell him. Eli left his backpack at school. Bo colored on his bedroom wall.

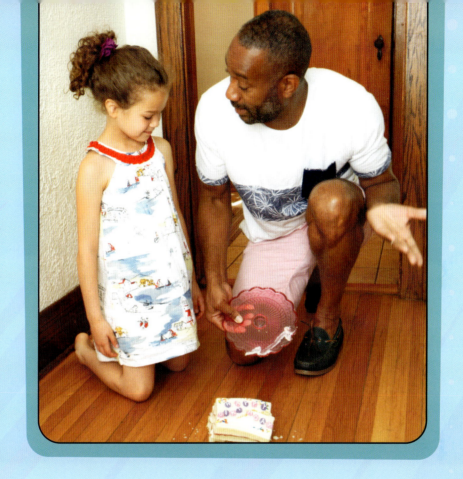

Grown-ups make mistakes too. They might spill or drop something. They could burn dinner or forget a friend's birthday. Maybe they get mad too quickly.

## OWNING UP

When you own up, you **admit** your mistake. You say that you were wrong. This can be hard to do. Why? No one likes to be wrong. It does not feel good. It could make you feel embarrassed or sad. You might be scared of getting into trouble. You might worry that people will not like you. It is OK to feel these **emotions**.

It can feel scary to admit you made a mistake. Maybe you don't want to talk about it. Or you might tell people that you didn't do it. Some people make **excuses**. Other people **blame** someone else.

You can learn to admit your mistakes. Being **honest** is a healthy way to live. You can be **responsible** for what you say and do. People will **respect** you and trust you.

## FACING YOUR MISTAKES

After you make a mistake, you might feel upset. First, try to **calm** down. Be patient with yourself. Take a break. Relax and breathe. It is easier to think when you are calm.

When you feel better, think about your mistake. What happened? What were you doing and thinking? Try to find out where things went wrong. Talk to a friend or family member about what happened.

Next, think about how you can fix things. What could you do next time? Plan how you will be better. Ask for help with your plan.

Be patient with yourself as you fix your mistake. Sometimes it takes a few tries to get it right. Do not give up!

Remember to think about other people. When you made your mistake, did it affect anyone? Think about how they might feel. Did you hurt their feelings? Own up to that. This takes courage. Tell them you are sorry. Ask them to forgive you. Tell them you will do better next time.

## DOING YOUR BEST

It is not easy to admit mistakes. But some good things come from mistakes. You learn how to solve problems. You learn to make new choices. You will have **confidence** to try new things.

Focus on what you have learned. Always do your best. Then you will feel better when you face your fear of admitting mistakes.

# THINKING RINGS

When you admit to a mistake, you will think through a few steps. Making some thinking rings can help you see these steps. This can help lessen your fear of admitting mistakes.

### What You Need

- different colors of construction paper
- scissors
- tape or stapler

### What You Do

1. Using blue, green, yellow, red, and pink pieces of paper, cut one long strip of each color.

2. Tape or staple the ends of each strip together. Now you have five big rings.

3. First, put the blue ring on your wrist. The blue ring stands for the things you can learn from your mistake. Think of two things you might learn from your mistake.

4. Now put the green ring on your wrist. This ring stands for your plan. How will you fix things? How will you do better next time?

5. Put on the yellow ring and the red ring. The yellow ring stands for the good things about your plan. Can you name some good things? The red ring stands for the negative things about your plan. Can you think of some negative things? Is your plan too big to do? Is your plan hard to understand?

6. Next, put on the pink ring. Ask yourself how you feel about admitting your mistake. Remember that there are no wrong answers.

# GLOSSARY

**admit** (ad-MIT)—to agree that something is true

**blame** (BLAYM)—to hold someone else responsible for something that happened

**calm** (KAHM)—to be quiet and peaceful

**confidence** (KON-fuh-duhns)—a feeling that you can do well

**emotion** (i-MOH-shuhn)—a strong feeling; people have and show emotions such as happiness, sadness, fear, and anger

**excuse** (EX-kus)—a reason you give to explain a mistake or why you have done something wrong

**honest** (ON-ist)—to be truthful; people who are honest do not lie

**mistake** (muh-STAKE)—something done in the wrong way

**respect** (ri-SPEKT)—to believe in the quality and worth of others and yourself

**responsible** (ri-SPON-suh-buhl)—doing what you say you will do

# READ MORE

Finne, Stephanie. *Making Good Decisions*. Minneapolis: Jump!, Inc., 2021.

Morlock, Rachael. *Overcoming Obstacles: Identifying Problems*. New York: PowerKids Press, 2020.

Taylor, Charlotte. *I Say I'm Sorry*. New York: Gareth Stevens Publishing, 2021.

# INTERNET SITES

*KidsHealth: Saying You're Sorry*
kidshealth.org/en/kids/sorry.html

*Wonderopolis: Can You Learn From Your Mistakes*
wonderopolis.org/wonder/Can-You-Learn-from-Your-Mistakes

## INDEX

admitting, 8, 10, 18
blaming, 10
choices, 18
emotions, 8
excuses, 10

feelings, 4, 8, 10, 12, 16, 18
forgiveness, 16
honesty, 10
planning, 14

## ABOUT THE AUTHOR

Mari Schuh's love of reading began with cereal boxes at the kitchen table. Today she is the author of hundreds of nonfiction books for beginning readers. Mari lives in the Midwest with her husband and their sassy house rabbit. Learn more about her at marischuh.com.